PILLOW

THE DOG WHO SAVED MY LIFE

May your Treat Jar Never Be Empty. *Debora*

To Jayden, Mitch, Derek, and my fur friends,
You have left your prints on my heart.

BY DEBORA DE SANTANNA
ART BY PENCIL MASTER STUDIO

Distribution by
KDP Amazon and Ingram Spark
P.O.D.

Printed in the United States of America and Canada
Title: Pillow: The Dog Who Saved My Life
Author: Debora De Santanna
Illustrator: Pencil Master Studio
Publicity: Talk+Tell

ISBNs
Hardcover: 978-1-7775573-0-0
Paperback: 978-1-7775573-2-4
EBook: 978-1-7775573-1-7

Publisher: Pillow the Dog Books Company
www.pillowthedog.com
Publisher's Cataloging-in-Publication data

Description: Toronto, ON: Pillow the Dog Books Company, 2021
Subjects: LCSH: Dogs--Juvenile fiction. | Friendship--Juvenile fiction. | Animal rescue--Juvenile fiction. | Pet adoption--Juvenile fiction. | CYAC Dogs--Fiction. | Friendship--Fiction. | Animal rescue--Fiction. | Pet adoption--Fiction. | BISAC JUVENILE FICTION / Animals / Dogs

Classification: LCC PZ7.1 .D47 Pil 2021 | DDC [E]--dc23

Meet the characters

Mick
the younger brother

He is
Friendly, thoughtful, always generous, athletic, and funny

Favourite things
Ice cream, counting things, BMX bikes, and dogs

Dislikes
Chores, his older sister bossing him around, and bee stings

Pillow the Dog

He is
Fluffy, curious, loyal, and a problem solver

Favourite things
Eating, playing, napping, and sniffing

Dislikes
Fireworks and storms

Jenn
the older sister

She is
Stylish, smart, bossy, a loyal friend, and dramatic

Favourite things
Bubble baths, skiing, rock climbing, and hanging out with her friends

Dislikes
Spiders, beans , haircuts, and her younger brother pestering her

Mommy

She is
Caring, reliable, and loves to laugh out loud

Favourite things
Dancing, summer nights, and helping others

Dislikes
Messy rooms, okra, and mosquito bites

Daddy

He is
Trustworthy, strict, and good with numbers

Favourite things
Steak, cottage life, and sports

Dislikes
Seafood, taking pictures, and bad drivers

Introducing . . .

Have you ever seen a walking pillow?

I bet you haven't, but I have. His name is Pillow, and he's my dog.

Well, today I'm going to tell you the story of how Pillow and I met. But first, I should introduce you to my family. My name is Mick and I have an older sister named Jenn. I'm seven years old and I love scooters and BMX bikes.

Another thing you should know about me is that I like to count things. Everywhere I go, I look for things I can count. How many red cars are parked on the street? How often will Jenn say "literally" today? How many times will the church bell ring this afternoon? I can't help it—I just love counting things.

My sister Jenn thinks counting is silly, but I think it's a good way to pay attention to everything around me. Speaking of Jenn, she's a good friend and very smart. I ask her tons of questions all the time. Sometimes she's great and sometimes she annoys me, but usually we're a good team.

We live in a busy city with lots of cars and big buildings. We're a small family—just me, my sister, and Mommy and Daddy—and we live in a house on a quiet street.

The Accident

Today after school, I was walking with Mommy to the fruit store. I was pretty busy counting the squirrels on the way there. I saw two red squirrels, then a brown one going up a tree. That makes three squirrels and we still had a half block to go before we got to the store.

When we were crossing the street, I let go of Mommy's hand to pick up a pretty pebble on the ground. She turned back and yelled, "Hurry!" as a car rushed toward us. I don't think the driver could see me.

Out of nowhere, this dirty little dog jumped in front of the car. The driver saw him and slammed on the brakes. The car missed me by inches.

All at once, we all went a bit crazy.

The driver jumped out of the car and said, "I am so sorry! I didn't see you on the road."

Mommy ran to hug and comfort me. I was so scared and a bit stunned.

We all realized that this little stray dog had saved my life by jumping in front of the car to get the driver's attention.

I looked down at the smelly dog, and I felt so much love and gratitude toward him. But when I bent over to pat him, I noticed he was bleeding.

"Mommy, he's hurt! We need to help him."

I felt like crying. I was so worried—I didn't want anything bad to happen to him.

I held him in my arms, not caring how dirty or smelly he was, and I whispered, "Don't worry, little guy. We'll take care of you, I promise."

Rushing to the Animal Hospital

We all jumped in the driver's car and took the little dog to the animal hospital. I held him tightly on my lap and prayed hard, saying, "Please, please, please be well."

The drive to the hospital took like FOREVER. To distract myself, I counted the traffic lights on the way there. One yellow light, two green lights, and one red light, where we stopped. But I wondered, *Where is the hospital?*

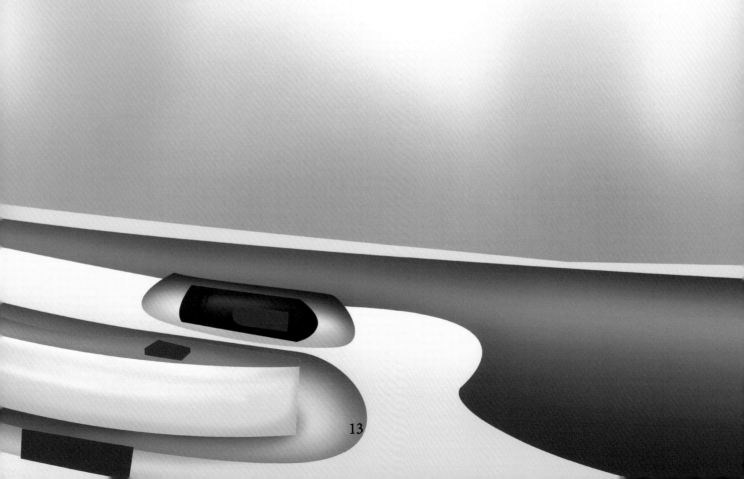

When we got there, my prayers were answered. After examining the puppy, the vet said, "You're a brave little dog, and very lucky too. You'll need three stitches in your paw, some love, a good meal, and a warm bath. Then you'll be as good as new."

I was so happy—the little dog would be okay! I started jumping up and down. I jumped so much that my mommy was worried I was going to hit my head.

I love you fur-ever!

16

A New Home

Mommy was very shaken and upset about the accident. She couldn't stop thinking that if it hadn't been for this smelly stray dog, this story wouldn't have had a happy ending.

Mommy looked at him and said, "I don't know how to repay you for saving my boy's life."

I looked at Mommy and said, "I know how we can repay him, Mommy."

"You do? How?"

"Let's take him home with us and give him love, food, a warm bath, and a family."

"Yes," Mommy said. "He deserves all that and more. But we can't take him home without checking if someone is looking for him, Mick. We need to make sure he's not a lost dog."

"But Mommy, I don't think he belongs to anyone. I think he's a stray dog. He's so skinny and so dirty!"

"I think Mick is right," said the vet. "This dog doesn't have a tag. He's not in the database of lost dogs and he looks like he's been on the streets for a while. I'm certain he was abandoned at a very young age. It's a miracle he survived on his own on the streets. This poor fellow needs a home and a loving family."

Mommy didn't need to be convinced any further. "We'll give him a new home and all the love he deserves."

I squeezed my new dog with happiness. I couldn't wait to get home and show my sister our new dog. Jenn was going to flip!

Dirty, Hungry, and Smelly

When we got home, my sister was in her room doing homework. She heard a yelp and came downstairs and said, "Where's that noise coming from?"

You really had to be there to see her face. She couldn't believe we'd returned home with a dog after just going out to get groceries. I had to tell her the story of the accident about ten times. Boy, did she have questions!

"Mick, are you hurt?" She looked at me, worried.

"No. I just got a big fright," I said.

"How old is the little dog?" Jenn asked.

19

"The vet says about eight months," I replied.

"Did the dog save your life?" she said.

"Yes. If the dog hadn't jumped in front of the car, the driver would have hit me instead," I said.

"Is it a boy dog or a girl dog?" Jenn asked.

"It's a boy dog," I replied.

"Why is he so dirty and smelly?" she said.

"He's a stray dog, Jenn. He didn't have anyone to take care of him before."

My sister felt very sad thinking about him alone on the streets, with no home and no one to look after him.

She helped me feed him. We didn't have any dog food yet, so Mommy said, "You can give him some dry cereal until I go to the store."

21

We gave him a full bowl of cereal, and he gobbled it up. So we gave him a second bowl, and he gobbled that up too. The little guy was so hungry!

My sister hugged him and immediately put him back on the floor. "Pee-ew. He needs a bath! He smells so bad. He's covered with dirt and muck. We don't even know what colour his fur is."

I knew Jenn was right, but I didn't like her saying all that in front of the little dog. He'd already had enough for one day, and I didn't want to hurt his feelings. My sister could be mean like that sometimes.

We took him to the bathroom and filled up the tub with warm water and lots of soap. He was so happy to take a bath.

I wondered how many times we'd have to wash him to get him really clean, so of course I started counting. We washed him once, and he still looked dirty and brownish. We filled up the tub a second time and washed him again, and he looked yellowish.

My sister didn't think that was his original colour, though. She thought he was still dirty and needed another bath. We gave him a third bath, and he looked beige. We gave him a fourth bath, and he was as white as snow.

"Maybe we should call him Snow," my sister said.

"But look at him, Jenn—he's as white as a feather pillow. I have the perfect name for him."

He looks like a Pillow!

25

"You do? What is it?" Jenn asked.

"His name should be Pillow. He looks like a pillow with four legs!" I replied.

My sister hugged our puppy and said, "You're right. He's long like a rectangle and rounded at the sides. And he's soft and fluffy—he feels like a pillow too."

Pillow really likes his name. Whenever we call him by it, he always runs toward us, wagging his tail.

And that, boys and girls, is the story of how Pillow got his name and how we started our lives together.

27

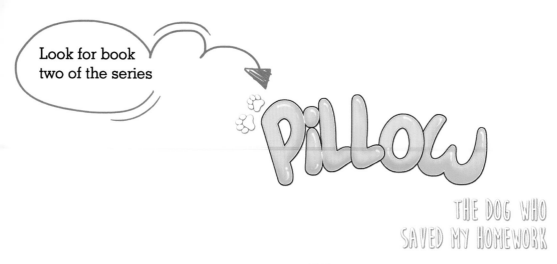

Look for book two of the series

PILLOW

THE DOG WHO SAVED MY HOMEWORK

Homework

This morning was such a rush in our house! I was late getting up. I was very tired and heard Mommy calling me from downstairs. "Sweetheart, it's time to get up. Brush your teeth and get dressed. We have to run today—Mommy's late for work!"

I really didn't want to get up. I wanted to stay in bed and not go to school. I was tired because I'd stayed up late last night finishing my English assignment. I had to write about three things I couldn't live without and why.

The thing is, I got this assignment weeks ago from Miss Margaret, but I didn't do it until last night. I should have known better—I was very stressed out trying to write it at the last minute. I worked very hard, but this morning I was nervous about the work I'd done. Did I do a good job? I wasn't so sure. I had a bit of a tummy ache thinking about it.

Debora de Santanna, Author

Debora De Santanna was born in Brazil and has spent most of her adult life in Canada. She began writing her children's stories about a dog named Pillow during the pandemic. They are based on the bedtime stories she told her children when they were little. Writing children's stories has always been Debora's passion, but having English as a second language was a huge hurdle for her, until an editor read her stories and encouraged her to publish them. When she's not writing, she can be found playing paddle tennis, working as a home stager, reading obsessively, or sharing a laugh with her friends. Debora lives in Toronto with her husband, two children, and their two adorable Labrador retrievers.

Pencil Master Digital Solutions Pvt. Ltd.

Pardeep Mehra is the founder of Pencil Master Digital Studio, a family-owned business employing a large group of talented artists providing end-to-end illustration and publishing services.

For more than 15 years, Pardeep has been providing his keen eye, visualization and digital art skills to create hundreds of beautifully illustrated books that delight children all over the world. Pardeep lives in India with his wife Priyam and daughter Mehar.

For more info and portfolio review, visit www.pencilmasterdigi.com

How the Pillow Stories Were Born

When my kids were little, we would all snuggle up in bed together for storytime. Evening was always my favourite time of the day, even after a long day when exhaustion had overcome me. But my unconditional love for my children would surface when I looked at their pink faces after their hot baths. With sleepy eyes, they would hug their pillows and say, "Mommy, tell us a story." Pillow the dog would appear in the stories every night. We could all imagine the fluffy white dog who had a special ability to solve each day's problems. Pillow was a lifesaver!

The Pillow stories are for every child who has been through a 'ruff' time, and they show how a pet can help children overcome life's challenges.

CERTIFICATE OF ADOPTION

This is to certify that

Mick

has officially adopted

Pillow

By signing this certificate I promise to give my dog a lifetime of love, care, attention, and fun! I promise to be his best friend forever.